Gabby
Drama Queen

To Olin,
Happy reading!

Joyce Grant

Gabby

Drama Queen

Joyce Grant

Illustrated by

Jan Dolby

Fitzhenry & Whiteside

Published in Canada by Fitzhenry & Whiteside, 195 Allstate Parkway, Markham, Ontario L3R 4T8

Published in the United States in 2013 by Fitzhenry & Whiteside, 311 Washington Street, Brighton, Massachusetts 02135

www.fitzhenry.ca   godwit@fitzhenry.ca

10 9 8 7 6 5 4 3 2 1

Library and Archives Canada Cataloguing in Publication
Grant, Joyce, 1963-, author
Gabby, drama queen / Joyce Grant ; illustrated by Jan Dolby.
ISBN 978-1-55455-310-5 (bound)
I. Dolby, Jan, 1967-, illustrator II. Title.
PS8613.R3653G333 2013   jC813'.6   C2013-904150-8

Publisher Cataloging-in-Publication Data (U.S.)
Grant, Joyce.
Gabby, drama queen / Joyce Grant ; illustrated by Jan Dolby.
[32] p. : col. ill. ; cm.
Summary: Gabby is setting up a stage for a play in her backyard with a friend. They're missing some crucial props, so Gabby shows that she can arrange letters from her magic letter book to create words that spell and transform into the props they need.
ISBN: 978-1-55455-310-5
1. Plays – Juvenile fiction. 2. Word games – Juvenile fiction. I. Dolby, Jan. II. Title.
[E] dc23 PZ7.G6358Ga 2013

Fitzhenry & Whiteside acknowledges with thanks the Canada Council for the Arts, and the Ontario Arts Council for their support of our publishing program. We acknowledge the financial support of the Government of Canada through the Canada Book Fund (CBF) for our publishing activities.

Cover and interior design by Daniel Choi
Cover image by Jan Dolby
Printed in China by Sheck Wah Tong Printing Press Ltd.

In loving memory of my father, Roy Grant.

—J.G.

For Jack and Georgia Mae, with all my love.

—J.D.

We wish to thank Grand Chief Eddie Erasmus,
Tlicho government, and Dr. John B. Zoe, Senior
Advisor to the Tlicho government, for their
invaluable assistance and guidance.
Thank you also to Dale Matasawagon of the
Assembly of First Nations.

Gabby and Roy were having fun. What could they do next?

"I know!" said Gabby. "We'll put on a play!"

"That's a great idea," said Roy.

Gabby ran inside and when she came out again, she was dressed like a queen. She swirled and twirled. Her taffeta gown made a satisfying *swish*.

"Our play will take place in a royal court," she announced.

"This is how we can make a stage." Gabby held up her special storybook.

To Roy's surprise, she threw it onto the grass!

The letters *bounced* right out of the book!

Gabby wasn't surprised. She knew that letters could make words—and words could make things. Useful things.

Gabby clicked together an **s** and a **t**.

She added an **a** that she found near an anthill,

a **g** that was on the grass,

and
a
teeny
tiny
e

that was hooked right on her earring.

She'd made a **stage**.

"Wow!" said Roy. He thought for a moment.

"I can be a swordfish!" he said. "I've always wanted to be a swordfish."

A swordfish? Fish didn't belong with queens!

Roy should play a court jester. Or maybe a king. Or at the very least, a prince.

A swordfish would ruin the whole play!

But Roy was excited.

He had already put on a gray toque he'd found.

On the front of it, he fastened a foam sword.

Gabby looked at him. He really *did* make a fine swordfish.

But still...

Roy started gathering letters.

He found a **c** and an **r** and clicked them together.

He added **o**, **w** and **n**.

"Cuh-Rrrr-OW-Nnnn," he said. "For you, Your Highness."

He placed the crown on Gabby's head.

"It fits perfectly!" said Gabby. Now she felt truly majestic.

Gabby had to admit, Roy always knew how to make a good game better.

The crown gave Gabby an idea. Suddenly she knew exactly how a swordfish could help a queen in a royal court.

"Let's make a stream for you," she told Roy. "A royal stream for a royal swordfish."

Together, the two actors found an **s** and a **t** and clicked them together. They added **r**, **e**, **a**, and **m**.

The little stream bubbled and burbled and twinkled in the sunshine.

splash!

stream

"The only thing we're missing is an audience," said Queen Gabriella.

"What's all this?" asked Gabby's neighbour.

"Mrs. Oldham!" the children cried.

Mrs. Oldham walked right past them.

Where was she going?

Now the stage had a curtain—

perfect!

Then, Mrs. Oldham found a comfy chair where she could watch the play unfold.

The audience fell silent. The curtains parted and the drama began.

The Perils of Queen Gabriella

Queen Gabriella swanned dramatically onto the stage. She looked miserable.

"I have looked everywhere for my crown!" she wailed. "I cannot find it. Without my crown, how can I be the queen?"

Suddenly, out of the royal moat, there was a mighty splash!

Rising from the water was the royal swordfish. And over its snout...was a crown.

"My crown," said the queen. "You found it! Now I can be a proper queen again."

The royal swordfish made happy swordfish noises when Gabby put the crown on her head.

"And they lived happily ever after!" announced Queen Gabriella.

The audience cheered. The actors took a bow.

"I'll bet we've all worked up a royal appetite," said Gabby. "What would everyone like to eat?"

Gabby shook her book. She snapped together two letters: **c** and **r**. She found some more letters...

...and made a delicious word...

Immediately, there was a plate of English crumpets, clotted cream, jam and tea, fit for a queen…and all of her loyal subjects.

There are two kinds of letters in the alphabet:

Vowels
A, E, I, O, U (and sometimes Y) are vowels. All the other letters in the alphabet are called consonants.

Consonants
These letters are consonants:
bcdfghjklmnpqrstvwxz and sometimes y.

Consonant blends
Some consonants work well together, like
S and T in **st**ick
C and R in **cr**umpet
S, P and L in **spl**ash.
These "blends" are like short-cuts for new readers. As you read aloud, focus on the words that have blends.

Fun Gabby: Drama Queen Activities—*For You!*

Find the **Birdie**

Did you notice the little bird on nearly every page? She's holding letters. Put them together to discover Gabby's royal name.

Queen Gabriella

How to Draw **Roy**

Draw:
- a circle for his head and two circles for his ears
- a rectangle for his body
- two triangles for his legs.

Add:
- spiky hair
- two triangles for his arms.

Erase the extra line across his face.

Add:
- eyes, nose, mouth, and cheeks
- hands and feet.

Add:
- a medicine wheel to his t-shirt
- zigzag trim
- an earring.

Write a Silly Story
- Using the blends in "The Queen's Crown" game, think of some words that start with blends. For instance: *tree, struggled, drip, green, plastic, climb, sweat.*
- Create a silly story or sentence using as many of the words as you can. For instance: Her forehead *dripped* with *sweat* as she *struggled* to *climb* the *green plastic tree.*

ABCDEFGHIJKLMNOPQRSTUVWXYZ

The Queen's Crown – a game to play alone or with friends.

Help Queen Gabriella find her crown!

1. Find something like a coin or a button to use as a place marker.
2. On your turn, flip a coin. If it lands on "heads," move your marker one space. If it lands on "tails," move two spaces.
3. Say the consonant blend out loud and say a word that begins with that sound.
4. Count the number of turns it took for you to reach the crown.

Visit Gabby's Website
For lots of free printable word games and activities, go to www.fitzhenry.ca/Gabby.

Nice Dice

For an extra challenge!

- As you land on each square, roll a die.
- Say the consonant blend—and then try to say as many words as the number on the die.
- For example, if you land on ST and roll a 3, you might say, "stream, stop, stuck!"

For a printable version of this gameboard, go to Gabby's website at www.fitzhenry.ca/Gabby.

Roy's T-Shirt
Roy's favourite t-shirt has a **medicine wheel** on it. It is a symbol in indigenous North American culture associated with astronomy, healing and teaching. It also symbolizes the interconnectedness of all beings on Earth.

Game board blends: pl tr gr s cr n str br sh pr d fl spl

abcdefghijklmnopqrstuvwxyz